# This book belongs to

CW00746287

.............................................

# For Anna and Charlie

© Nicky Nash 2020  @nickycnash1

All rights reserved.

# With special thanks to:

Louise Gribbons, for sharing her inspirational poem
and giving me permission to adapt it in this way.

**'The Day We Spring-Cleaned The World'**
is featured within.

Emma Lamb, who first gave me the
idea to create a book for our children.

Darren Ammar, for helping me
produce the final version of this book.

# OUR WORLD NEEDS A CLEAN

Created by
Nicky Nash

The world that we live in is busy.
There are people all around.
All of these people carry tiny germs,
Which go into the air and onto the ground.

Some of these germs grew bigger,
They wanted to stay and play.
They didn't want to hurt anyone.
But they wouldn't go away.

Sometimes, germs try to ride on your hand.
Or tickle your throat or nose.
They can make you cough and sneeze.
And make your cheeks as red as a rose.

And as these germs grew bigger,
They started to make people ill.
And with every cough we coughed,
More of these germs would spill.

All the Queens and Kings were worried,
"It's time to clean the world up!" They said.
And so they had to close some fun places,
Just so these germs couldn't spread.

So, for a while, we can't go to the park,
Or have our friends round for tea.
We'll have to ring all our friends instead,
As strange as this may be.

Instead of going to Soft Play,
We'll make our own fun inside.
Who knows what adventures we'll have.
And we'll soon be back on the slide.

While we're busy having all this fun,
The world will be getting a clean.
Perhaps with a great big scrubbing brush,
It will be the cleanest it's ever been!

Our nursery will be so sparkly,
The library will shimmer and shine,
The farm will look so lovely and clean,
That we'll want to go all the time!

And the germs will grow smaller and smaller,
And soon the Kings and Queens will decide,
That it's time to re-open the fun places,
So we can all play together outside.

Our friends will come round to play again.
We will splash in the swimming pool.
We'll be able to go back to nursery,
And the big children will go back to school.

And when things are back to normal,
One day, you might ask, "Is this story true?"
And I will hold your hand tightly and say,
"It is, but our love got us through."

# The Day We Spring-Cleaned The World

## by Louise Gribbons

The world it got so busy,
There were people all around.
They left their germs behind them;
In the air and on the ground.

These germs grew bigger and stronger.
They wanted to come and stay.
They didn't want to hurt anyone -
They just really wanted to play.

Sometimes they tried to hold your hand,
Or tickled your throat or your nose.
They could make you cough and sneeze
And make your face as red as a rose.

And so these germs took over.
They started to make people ill,
And with every cough we coughed
More and more germs would spill.

All the queens and kings had a meeting.
"It's time to clean the world up!" they said.
And so they had to close lots of fun stuff,
Just so these germs couldn't spread.

We couldn't go to cinemas
Or restaurants for our tea.
There was no football or parties,
The world got as quiet as can be.

The kids stopped going to school,
The mums and dads went to work less.
Then a great, big, giant scrubbing brush
Cleaned the sky and the sea and the mess!

Dads started teaching the sums,
Big brothers played with us more,
Mums were in charge of homework
And we read and played jigsaws galore!

The whole world was washing their hands
And building super toilet roll forts!
Outside was quiet and peaceful,
Now home was the place for all sports.

So we played in the world that was home
And our days filled up with fun and love,
And the germs they grew smaller and smaller
And the sun watched from up above.

Then one morning the sun woke up early,
She smiled and stretched her beams wide.
The world had been fully spring cleaned,
It was time to go back outside!

We opened our doors oh so slowly
And breathed in the clean and fresh air.
We promised thar forever and always
Of this beautiful world we'd take care!

This book was put together with uncertainty, trepidation, and a lot of love. It was made in the hope that it would help my daughter understand the huge changes brought to her life by the Coronavirus pandemic.

– Nicky Nash –

**Thank you to every NHS staff member
and volunteer. For everything.**

All profits made from the sale of this book will go
directly to NHS Charities COVID-19 Urgent Appeal.

Further donations can be made here

**https://uk.virginmoneygiving.com/OurWorldNeedsAClean**

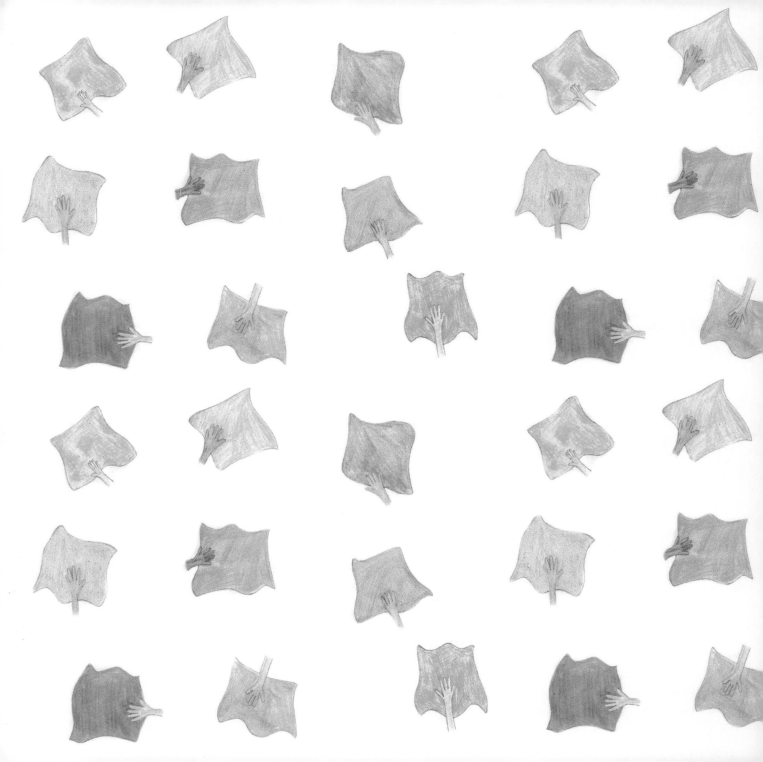

Printed in Great Britain
by Amazon

40760305R00015